This Little Tiger book belongs to:

_____

_____

_____

For Gussie, forever in our hearts ... -TC

For Piddle Valley Preschool - JC

LITTLE TIGER PRESS
1 The Coda Centre
189 Munster Road, London SW6 6AW
www.littletiger.co.uk
First published in Great Britain 2010
This edition published 2016
Text copyright © Tracey Corderoy 2010
Illustrations copyright © Jane Chapman 2010
Visit Jane Chapman at www.ChapmanandWarnes.com
Tracey Corderoy and Jane Chapman have asserted their rights
to be identified as the author and illustrator of this work
under the Copyright, Designs and Patents Act, 1988
All rights reserved

ISBN 978-1-84869-519-1
2 4 6 8 10 9 7 5 3 1

The Little White Owl

Tracey Corderoy   Jane Chapman

LITTLE TIGER PRESS
London

Once there was a little white owl who lived by himself in the snow. He didn't have a mommy. He didn't have a daddy. He didn't **even** have a name.

But he didn't really mind too much.
It had **always** been like that.
And his head was full
of happy stories.

Sometimes he was a brave white knight . . .

and sometimes he was a snowflake.

Sometimes he was a rocket, blasting off to the moon!

But every night, at bedtime, he sat on his **favorite** branch, nibbling toast spread with strawberry jam and counting the stars, by himself.

Then one day, he looked at the big, blue sky that stretched on and on forever . . .

"I wonder what's out there?" said the little white owl.

So he packed his teddy and his clock. It was time to see the world!

For days the little white owl flew—
over turquoise oceans and deserts of gold.
Then he spotted the **prettiest** trees,
sprinkled with tiny jewels, so down, down,
down he swooped—**but wait** . . .

. . . these jewels had beaks! They were owls—
beautiful owls! Owls just like him!
"Would anyone like a bite of toast?" he said.

But the beautiful owls sat quiet and still.
They didn't want to spoil their perfect feathers.
"How very **plain** you are," groaned the green.
"No colors at all," sniffed the dotty red.
"You don't belong with us. GO AWAY!"

"But I **do** have colors!" cried the little white owl. "**Here**—in my heart! And bumping up and down in me are lots of happy stories. I'll share them with *you* if you want me to?"

The owls sat and thought, then.
"Hmmm . . ." sighed the blue.
"A story might help pass the time."
"Fine, but just one," said
the flowery pink with a yawn.

So the little white owl swung on
a branch with his little teddy.
And he munched his toast and
shared a happy story.

"Aaahhhhh . . ." breathed
the blue owl dreamily when the
little white owl had finished.
The other owls all glared at her.
"Ooops, sorry!" she blushed.
"But couldn't we have just one more?"

So the little white owl closed his eyes and magical stories came pouring from his heart. Colorful tales of castles and knights and dragons with fiery breath . . .

and blasting through
moonbeams and counting
bright stars and tumbling
down like a snowflake!

Slowly, and rather to their surprise, the owls began to smile. "Aaahhhhh . . ." they breathed. Then suddenly, "MORE!" everyone cried.

At last, when all his toast was gone, the little white owl checked his clock. "Gosh, I need to go!" he gasped. "Back to my sparkly home. I need to feel the snow and count the stars . . ."

But then . . .

...a blue wing fluttered
and a tail of dotty red
began to twitch...

"Take us too!" cried the pretty owls, sweeping into the sky. "We want to feel your fluffy snow and count your sparkly stars. And play . . . and laugh . . . and tumble—just like you!"

So the little white owl led them home
where they tumbled and twirled on the ice.
Like splashes of rainbow they speckled
the snow, their colors brighter than ever!

Later, they huddled together and sipped warm cocoa.
"Tomorrow, when we fly home," said the blue,
"the white clouds will remind us of you! Promise
you'll visit very soon?"

"I promise," smiled the little white owl,
"and you can tell me all **your** stories."
Then he snuggled up on his
favorite branch . . .

. . . and soon was dreaming happy dreams, as a huge, silver moon lit the deep, dark sky that stretched on and on **forever**.